TWICE
TOLD
TALES

Twicetold Tales is published by Stone Arch Books
A Capstone Imprint
1710 Roe Crest Drive
North Mankato, Minnesota 56003
www.capstonepub.com

Library of Congress Cataloging-in-Publication Data
Snowe, Olivia, author.
  The glass voice / by Olivia Snowe; illustrated by
Michelle Lamoreaux.
      pages cm. -- (Twicetold tales)
  Summary: In this modern version of Cinderella,
Chantella Verre is being treated like a servant by her
oblivious father's new wife and her awful twins—but
Chantella gets a chance to sing at the Next Teen Star
audition when her former nanny shows up to set
things right.
  ISBN 978-1-4342-9148-6 (library binding) -- ISBN
978-1-4342-9152-3 (pbk.) -- ISBN 978-1-4965-0085-4
(ebook)
1. Cinderella (Tale)--Juvenile fiction. 2. Fairy tales.
3. Stepdaughters--Juvenile fiction. 4. Fathers and
daughters--Juvenile fiction. 5. Women singers--
Juvenile fiction. [1. Fairy tales. 2. Stepfamilies--Fiction.
3. Singing--Fiction.] I. Lamoreaux, Michelle, illustrator.
II. Title.
  PZ8.S41763Gl 2014
  [Fic]--dc23
                          2013045706

Designer: Kay Fraser
Vector Images: Shutterstock

Printed in China.
032014   8116WAIF14

The Glass Voice

by Olivia Snowe

illustrated by Michelle Lamoreaux

STONE ARCH BOOKS™

You know the story.

You've heard it before.

Everyone has.

Now, read it again.

A new twist. A new gasp.

The story is told again.

TWICETOLD.

Chantella Verre sat in the dressing room in the church and sniffled. She ran her fingers over the green velvety fabric of the couch.

"No more crying," she mumbled. She lifted her chin and found her reflection in the mirror on the dressing table.

"Ugh, I look awful," she said to herself. Her eyes were red and swollen. Makeup ran down her cheeks. She stepped into the bathroom, blew her nose, and wiped the smeared makeup from her face.

Then she heard a knock on the door. "You in there, Chantella?" her dad said. He stuck his head in as she came out of the bathroom.

"Hi, Dad," she said, doing her best to cover up the crying in her voice and the runny in her nose. She sat on the couch again and tried to smile for him—he *had* just gotten married after all—but it turned to a sobbing hiccup.

Her dad sighed and walked into the room. He squatted in front of his daughter—*of course he wouldn't sit down next to me,* Chantella thought—and put a hand on her knee.

"You're upset," he said, barely glancing her way. He never looked her in the eyes anymore.

"I miss Mom," she said. "I'm sorry."

Her dad sighed again. "I miss her, too," he said. "And when I look at you, I miss her doubly."

She took her dad's hand. He flinched a little as their hands touched. "You're her all over again," her dad said, his voice and eyes soft and caring. They almost never were nowadays. He looked at Chantella and pushed a chestnut lock of hair behind her ear. But Chantella knew he wasn't seeing his daughter. He was seeing his late wife.

She coughed, and her dad's trance ended. He cleared his throat and stood up. "That's over now," he said, tugging at the lapels of his tuxedo. "Now we have Mara and the twins. A new family. It'll be a fresh start."

But I don't want a fresh start, Chantella thought as he left, closing the door behind him.

Chantella followed him out a moment later, but rather than heading to the front of the church to throw rice and cheer with the rest of the guests, she went out the side door into a small, serene graveyard. From there, Chantella could hear the cheers as her dad and new stepmother hurried out the ornate doors and down the steps to their waiting limousine. She could picture them both smiling and running, crouched against the rice that was raining down on them.

She stepped gently past graves, old and new, and stopped at one of the newest. It shined. Its letters were still sharp and crisp: *Cordelia Verre, beloved wife and mother. She is singing in heaven.*

Chantella was tired of crying. Her mother had died a little less than a year earlier, and she had been crying ever since. But today was the worst day in a long time. Standing at her mother's grave, listening to her family and friends applauding in front of the church, she thought she might cry again. But instead, she sang. *"You are my sunshine, my only sunshine."*

Her mother used to sing it to her at bedtime and bath time. When Chantella felt she was too old to be sung to like a baby, she asked her mom to stop. She was probably twelve then—just three years ago. Now she wished she'd never asked her mom to stop singing.

2

Chantella sang the whole song right there in the graveyard, and when she was done, she was still crying. "My sunshine is gone," Chantella whispered to the stone, placing her hand on its cold, hard face. "I miss you, Mommy."

"She's gone completely insane," said a voice from behind her. It was Mara's son, Colin. And that surely meant Colin's twin, Colleen, was there as well.

"Talking to dead people," Colleen said, nearly cackling. "Twisted."

"Go away," Chantella said. It took all her effort to hold back more tears.

"Happily," Colin said. He leaned toward her, though, and added in a whisper, "We'll see you in the limo, sis."

With that, her new stepsiblings departed, laughing as they went. Now that she was alone with her mother, Chantella let the tears flow again.

* * *

Chantella couldn't linger in the cemetery much longer. From the corner, she could see her dad's long silver limo as it pulled away from the curb. Behind it flew a ghastly banner: *Just Married*. And with that, her father's limousine was gone—headed to the reception.

Still at the curb was a black limo, its back door wide open so the twins could take their places. The driver was waiting for her to climb into the back with those miserable twins. If she didn't get there soon, she could only imagine what lie the twins might tell him so they could leave without Chantella.

She pushed through the creaky iron gate of the cemetery and headed for the front of the church. *I hope we don't get stuck in traffic,* Chantella thought as she headed toward the limo. She was sure she could only stand the twins in doses of five minutes or less.

For once, Chantella was glad her father's work schedule was so hectic. He wasn't going to take a honeymoon with Mara, which meant she wouldn't be stuck at home alone with the twins.

She sighed as the crowd of well-wishers began to thin, heading for their cars, and she quickened her pace to reach the limo before the twins could convince the driver to leave her behind.

Before she reached the door, though, she

felt a hand touch her shoulder. Chantella was too upset to be friendly. It was no doubt one of her dad's friends or business partners, ready to offer hearty congratulations. She closed her eyes and took a deep breath to brace herself. Then she put on her best fake smile, opened her eyes, and turned around.

"Hello, little wonder," said the woman in front of her. She was around Chantella's height, and about ten years older, with startlingly red hair worn high on her head. Suddenly, Chantella's fake smile turned real . . . an ear-to-ear, shining grin.

"Verna!" she shouted with glee. She threw her arms around the woman's neck.

"My!" Verna exclaimed, her voice a pleasing mix of surprise and joy. "I never expected anyone to be so happy to see me!"

Chantella released the woman—her former nanny, whom she hadn't seen in five years, the last time Mom had gone on international tour.

"I'm sorry," Chantella said, smiling now, in spite of the tears still on her cheeks. "I didn't know Dad had invited you!"

"He didn't," Verna said. Then she leaned closer and whispered, "The truth is, dear, I'm not here for your father."

"No?" Chantella said.

Verna shook her head. "I'm here for you."

"Oh, then you shouldn't have come," Chantella said. "I hate this. I wish it wasn't happening."

"But that's why I came," Verna said. "To see how you were doing."

Chantella had always liked her nanny. She had spent nearly every afternoon with the young woman—a college student then—and occasionally stretches of days when her mother was on tour and her father was busy or out of town on a business trip.

Verna was a wonderful role model for

Chantella. They had roamed the little city on the river together, sometimes on busy streets, in and out of candy stores, ice cream shops, bookstores, and museums, sometimes on the banks of the big river, their pants rolled up to their knees, their shoes and socks safe and dry on the footpath, while they splashed ankle-deep in the ice-cold, crystal-clear shallows.

Chantella had loved her nanny then, and seeing her now, on this horrible afternoon, she realized she loved her still. But—and it troubled Chantella to think it—there had always been something a little off about the young woman.

She sensed it even now. It was a glimmer in Verna's eyes—a grayish blue: pale and not quite human. It was a lilt in her voice, like she'd come from a land far away—a place not on maps.

Verna took Chantella's hand. "You should hurry now," she whispered. "Those two stinkers won't wait much longer."

Chantella sighed. "Perhaps I'll just go to the reception with you," she said. "I'd prefer it to going with them, and it will give us a chance to catch up."

"No," Verna said. "I'm not going to the reception. I merely stopped by to check up on my favorite former charge. But I will drop by sometime, and we can catch up then. If that's all right with you . . . ?"

"I'd love it," Chantella said. She hugged Verna again. "I should hurry. Thank you, V!"

With that, she turned and hurried toward the idling limousine. As she reached the car, the limo driver hopped out and opened the door for her.

"Finally," said Colleen, as Chantella slid across the seat. The twins sat across from her, their arms crossed and their faces grim and angry.

Colin leaned forward and banged on the divider the moment the driver was back behind the wheel. "Let's go!" he snapped. The limo pulled away from the curb.

Chantella looked out the window as they slid past the length of the church.

Verna still stood there, and though the limousine windows were darkly tinted, she seemed to hold Chantella's eyes as the car passed.

~ 3 ~

Chantella kept to herself during the reception. She was envious of how well the twins were handling their mother's second wedding. "Don't they miss their father?" she muttered, her elbow on the table and her chin on her fist.

She watched them dance, saw them sneak extra desserts, and spotted them teasing a distant cousin for not being married.

The new family went home to the Verre

estate late that night. It was an old and impressive home that sat atop a wooded hill. It had a remarkable view from up there—you could look down on the river on one side and over the city's downtown on the other.

Mara and the twins would be moving their things in the next day, and Chantella dreaded it. The new Verre family entered the house and almost immediately they all kicked off their shoes, fell onto couches and easy chairs, and sighed, happy to be home.

All except Chantella. Over the last year, she'd often thought that the big house, with only two occupants (who were both often very sad) was a lonely place.

At one point, she might have thought a pair of siblings would be a welcome addition. Then she met Colleen and Colin and their dreadful mother. A big, empty house for just Chantella and her dad seemed like heaven now.

"We'll each have our own room," Colleen

said as she fluffed up some pillows on the couch and grabbed a blanket to cover her legs.

Chantella sat on the end of the couch as she listed the house's bedrooms in her mind: there was her father's huge master suite, there was her own bedroom down the hall from it, and there was the spare bedroom—the one Mom had used as her music room—at the far end of the hall. There were rooms that Chantella's dad used as libraries, offices, and game rooms, but she knew he wouldn't give those up.

That's only three bedrooms, Chantella thought, *and I'm certainly not giving up mine.*

"You certainly will," Mara announced, responding to Colleen. "I won't have my children sharing a room in a house so tremendous."

Chantella was about to protest when Mara continued. "Naturally Chantella will be happy to give up her room for one of her new siblings," she said.

"Where am I supposed to sleep?" Chantella asked the group, sitting up in shock. "That's been my bedroom since—well, since forever!"

"Now, Chantella," her father said. His voice was tired—tired of sadness, tired of grieving, and tired of Chantella's complaining.

"You get the best room of all, dear," Mara said, standing up. She walked across the living room and dropped onto the couch beside Chantella. She even put an arm around her. "You'll have all the privacy you can dream of—your own bathroom and even a sitting area."

Chantella's face turned white. "The maid's quarters?" she said. She launched herself off the couch and stomped across the living room and then turned around to face her stepmother. "You're putting me in the maid's quarters?"

Mara put her hand to her chest, aghast. "Why, Chantella," she said, "you act as if we've banished you to the unfinished part of the basement, or the garage!"

"Really, sweetie," her dad said. "It's the biggest room in the house, aside from the master suite. You'll have your own apartment."

Chantella opened her mouth to speak, but she could think of nothing to say. The truth was, the maid's quarters *were* spacious and private.

And I won't be anywhere near my new siblings or the bedroom that Dad will now share with Mara instead of Mom, Chantella thought. *And it will be perfect for practicing singing.*

"Fine," Chantella said, instead of protesting further. "I'll go get some of my stuff."

"Oh, it's already taken care of, dear," Mara said. "I took the liberty of asking a few of the men from your father's warehouse to come move some of your things during the wedding."

"You *what?*" Chantella said. "You moved my stuff already?"

Mara leaned back and crossed her legs.

"You'll be quite comfortable," she said, and she busied herself examining the state of her manicure.

Chantella glared at Mara, and then flashed an angry glance at her father. He only held her eyes for a moment before looking down at the carpet.

As Chantella marched out of the living room, Colleen and Colin cackled behind her. She waited until she was down the hall and out of their sight before she wiped a tear from her cheek.

* * *

That first night in her new "apartment" was long. Every creak of the floor was new. The maid's quarters were next to the kitchen, and the refrigerator's constant whir and occasional clicks and thuds haunted her, making her toss and turn for half the night.

It was nearly three in the morning when Chantella finally threw off her blanket and found the plastic tub that held her CD collection. Most of them had been her mom's. Since her mother died, however, Chantella had added quite a few finds of her own.

One in particular, though, was the object of Chantella's hunt through the bin, and she found it near the bottom. Its case featured a photo of the most beautiful woman Chantella had ever known: her mother. Chantella pulled the disc out and put it on.

Then she lay on her bed again and eventually drifted off to sleep, her mother's soothing voice serenading her with haunting, jazzy notes that drowned out the odd creaks and the hum of the refrigerator.

~4~

Chantella was the first one to wake up. She hadn't slept very well, even with the company of her mother's voice. It was barely six o'clock when she found her robe and dragged herself to the kitchen.

"I can't believe it's Monday," she mumbled as she filled the teapot with water and put it on the stovetop to boil. It had been an exhausting weekend. Chantella could hardly believe she had to be at school in less than two hours.

The house seemed quiet. Chantella didn't hear any footsteps as she cracked two eggs and beat them with a whisk. No shower ran upstairs as she put two slices of whole wheat toast into the toaster and poured herself a mug of tea. No voices drifted down from the second floor as she poured the beaten eggs into a pan and pushed them over high heat until they scrambled.

But as Chantella moved the eggs from the pan to a plate, two pairs of footsteps thundered down the back stairway.

Before she knew it, the twins were charging into the kitchen, giggling. Colin snatched the plate of eggs and the fork from the counter. Colleen grabbed the slices of toast just as they popped up.

"Thanks a lot, Chantella," Colin said. He and Colleen each took a stool at the kitchen island and began to dig into Chantella's eggs and toast.

"That wasn't for—" Chantella began to protest. But Mara cut her off as she click-clacked into the kitchen.

"Ah!" she said. "Is my lovely stepdaughter fixing breakfast for her family this morning?" She sat beside her children and grinned at Chantella. "Just egg whites for me, please. And certainly no toast." She laughed as she reached for Chantella's mug of tea.

Chantella clenched her jaw and rinsed out the frying pan. "Is Dad coming down?" she asked. She brought the pan back to the stove and pulled the eggs from the fridge again.

Mara sighed grandly and said, "I'm sure my husband would rather stay upstairs. He'll come down after you've eaten and showered and left for school."

"Why?" Chantella said. She had a guess, but she couldn't bear to think it.

Mara had no such difficulty. "Oh, darling," she said, her voice thick with false sympathy, "you of all people know how hard the poor man has had it. He adored your mother—though I hardly know why. And she left him so utterly destroyed, as I'm sure you understand."

Chantella did understand—far too well.

"Poor thing," Mara went on. She sipped her tea. "He looks at you and sees her. No wonder he doesn't want to spend any time with you."

Chantella pushed the egg whites around the pan as she tightened her jaw, holding back tears. Although it hurt to hear, she wouldn't give them the satisfaction of seeing her upset.

When the eggs were done, she put them on a plate and passed them across the island to Mara. Then she left the kitchen and headed for her new bathroom.

Chantella stood in the shower and tried to sing, but at the first line, she croaked and sobbed instead.

★ ★ ★

Chantella had a hard time concentrating at school that day. She had given up trying to pay attention during third-period chemistry, the formulas on the whiteboard just swimming in front of her.

Mara's comments from that morning still stung, but Chantella knew that her wicked stepmom was lying. *Dad was probably showering, shaving, and dressing for work. Nothing unusual about that,* she thought.

Chantella managed to smile as she walked into the cafeteria for lunch. She looked forward to seeing her friends and complaining about her awful new stepsiblings.

Janis and Jaenelle—the J's—were at their usual table. But before she reached them, two more people sat down with their backs to her.

It couldn't be them, Chantella thought. But then they turned in their chairs and flashed open-mouthed smiles her way. *The twins.* Still, Chantella sat down in her usual spot.

"Hi, sis," Colleen said, then turned her attention back to the J's. "We're so thrilled to meet our new dear sister's *dearest* friends."

Colin cooed, "She's so *dear* to us. Why, do you know what she did this morning?" He cast a long, loving look at Chantella. She could tell that the J's weren't aware of Colin's sarcasm.

"She made breakfast!" Colleen said. "For me, Colin, *and* Mom. Isn't that wonderful?"

Colin put his hands on Chantella's. "What a great welcome to our new home," he said. "Can you believe we were nervous about moving in?"

Colleen nodded. "We sure were. And this delightful girl cooked eggs and toast for the whole family."

"Well," said Colin, "not the *whole* family. Dad didn't come downstairs till we'd left."

Chantella turned her face to the window. She looked out over the school grounds, unable to watch her awful stepsiblings any longer. The

J's couldn't pull themselves away. They leaned on the table, their lunches untouched, hanging on the twins' every word.

"Did you know she even gave up her bedroom?" Colleen said. "Just for me!"

"She sleeps in the maid's room now," Colin said, taking a bite of his pasta salad.

Colleen shifted suddenly to face her brother and gasped. "You know *what?*" she said, her smile wide and devious. "She sleeps in the maid's room, and she served us all breakfast this morning. She practically *is* the maid!"

The twins laughed so hard they buckled over in their seats, holding their stomachs. Even the J's twittered like birds. Unable to take it anymore, Chantella pushed her tray aside, got up, and left the cafeteria.

The school week was long and torturous. Chantella had managed to sneak out of the house on two mornings without serving anyone breakfast, but the other days were the same as Monday. On Friday morning, after she'd made scrambled eggs for her stepfamily, Chantella grabbed her books and headed for the front door.

At the last moment, though, she ran upstairs as quietly as she could manage and knocked urgently on the door to the master suite.

"Daddy?" she said in a frantic whisper. She hadn't seen her father all week. "It's Chantella. Can I come in?"

He didn't reply. Perhaps he was in the shower. But Chantella would never know, because at that moment, a long-fingered hand—more like a claw—gripped her shoulder. Chantella spun, facing her stepmom.

"How could you be so cruel?" the woman said as she leaned close to Chantella's startled face. Mara's long hair—a startling white-blond—hung in front of her shoulders.

"You know how much it hurts him to see you," Mara went on, "yet you keep trying to stick your detestable face in front of him."

"I—" Chantella said. "I don't mean to—"

"Get downstairs," Mara said, clasping her hands in front of her and straightening her spine. She cast her gaze past Chantella, as if she

was a duchess dismissing some lowly servant. "*My* children have already left for school. If you hurry, perhaps you won't be late."

★ ★ ★

The school day dragged. Classes seemed never-ending. Chantella couldn't focus on anything. In math, the numbers blurred together on the whiteboard. In English, words seemed to have no meaning at all.

Even the lunch period passed slowly. Chantella ate lunch at the end of a long table with people she didn't know. She refused to share the J's with the twins, and the J's, for whatever reason, seemed to like the twins. In fact, the J's hadn't even spoken to Chantella since her stepsiblings had befriended them.

When Chantella got home that afternoon, she found Mara sitting on the small couch in the maid's quarters. "Chantella," the woman said in her icy tone. "Sit with me a moment."

Chantella obeyed.

"I heard from your assistant principal, Ms. Paulsen, this afternoon," Mara said. She placed a hand on Chantella's knee. Chantella flinched at the touch.

"What for?" Chantella had never been in trouble in school before. Her grades had always been very good, too.

"It seems," Mara went on, "that you've been distracted this week. You missed some homework assignments."

"Oh," Chantella said. It was true. But with everything going on recently, surely it was forgivable just this once.

"You failed a pop quiz in math class this morning—were you aware of that?" Mara asked.

"I kind of had the feeling I didn't do well," Chantella said. "It's been a hard week."

"Well," Mara said, standing up and facing Chantella, her chin low and her manner condescending. "It ends now. As of this moment, you will focus on only two things: your schoolwork and your housework."

"Housework?" Chantella said.

"I've drawn up a list," the woman said, pulling it from behind her back and presenting it to Chantella. She went to the door and called out, "Colin! Come here, please!" as Chantella read the list of new duties: vacuuming, cooking, mopping, washing windows, cleaning toilets, doing laundry. The list went on and on.

"I don't understand," Chantella said. "This is a list of every chore in the house! Don't Colleen and Colin have to do any chores?"

"*My* children are not distracted in school," Mara said. "I haven't received a call from Ms. Paulsen about *my* children."

Colin stuck his head in the room. "You called, Mom?" he said.

"Chantella has been having some trouble focusing on her work. We're going to help her," Mara said.

Colin examined Chantella the way a hyena might examine a wounded antelope. "How?"

Mara went to Chantella's desk, closed her laptop, and handed it to Colin. "This will stay in the living room from now on," she said. "That way," she added, looking at Chantella, "we'll always know what you're up to when you're supposed to be working."

Chantella swallowed hard. Her laptop held dozens of MP3s and videos of her mother. She couldn't bear to see Mara and Colin handling it.

Colin slipped the laptop under his arm. "What else?" he said.

Mara stepped up to the plastic bin under the window. "This," she said, looking down at it. "When Chantella proves that she can focus on her studying, then we can consider letting her have music on while she does."

Colin hoisted the bin onto his hip and headed for the door.

"Wait!" Chantella said, grabbing Colin's

arm. "That has all my mom's music in it! Let me keep those CDs at least."

Mara scoffed. "Hardly," she said. "Those CDs *especially* have to go. I can think of no greater distraction—not only to you, but to the entire family—than your mother's warbling."

"Warbling?" Chantella yelled. "Warbling?!"

Mara clucked her tongue. "My, she's having a fit!" she said. She pulled Chantella's hand off Colin's arm—Mara was surprisingly strong—and the boy left the room.

"It's not fair!" Chantella shrieked.

"Fair," Mara said. Her tone made the word sound absurd. "The sooner you accept just how *unfair* things are about to get around here, the happier you'll be."

★ ★ ★

That night, after eating the supper Chantella had cooked, Mara stood up from the table full of dirty dishes.

"When you've finished cleaning up this mess," she said to Chantella as she patted the corners of her mouth with a napkin, "you will vacuum the media room."

"Quickly!" Colleen added. "My favorite show is on soon and I will not have you drowning it out with that awful vacuum cleaner."

Chantella clenched her jaw and stacked dirty plates as her stepfamily left the dining room. Her dad hadn't been to dinner, of course. She wasn't even sure he was home.

Does he know what Mara has been up to? she wondered. *Does he know I've been made a servant in my own house?*

Chantella filled the dishwasher, switched it on, and hurried to the media room with the vacuum. Colin and Colleen were already there, a bag of popcorn open on the couch between them, its oily contents spilling freely as they grabbed handful after handful.

"Finally," Colleen said. "You better hurry."

Chantella clicked on the vacuum and pushed it across the huge carpeted floor. "I don't see why you couldn't do this yourselves," she mumbled, "instead of stuffing your faces with popcorn."

Somehow Colin heard her over the roar of the vacuum. "Because our mother—who loves us dearly and enjoys spending time with us—is *alive*."

With that, he tossed a handful of popcorn, scattering the white and yellow puffs across the part of the carpet Chantella had already vacuumed. She rushed to finish the chore, with tears threatening to stream down her face.

Just as Colleen's show had come on, and Chantella was wrapping up the vacuum's cord, Mara found her.

"After you've put that away," Mara said, "you can polish the wood furniture in the formal living room."

"What?" Chantella said. "I thought I was done for the night. It's late. I have homework."

"It's Friday," Mara said. "You have the whole weekend for schoolwork. Do as you're told."

As Mara walked away, she said, "I don't believe the furniture in the living room has ever been polished. What miserable house your mother kept."

* * *

Chantella finished her chores late. After the living room furniture, there was the bathroom to scrub, the dishwasher to empty, and a load of laundry to start and finish. She crawled into bed with the rest of the house asleep.

"That witch didn't get everything," she whispered. She reached under her bed and pulled out a thick, old book: a collection of fairy tales.

She put it on her lap and quickly flipped through the pages till they stopped on their own. There, sandwiched between the pages, was a photograph of a beautiful young woman with chestnut curls and loving eyes. Chantella pulled the photo out, pressed it to her chest, and curled up in bed as she sang herself to sleep.

Chantella dreamed of her mother that night, just as she'd hoped she would. They sang together, and then her mother took Chantella's hands in her own and said, "He loves you. He'll remember. You might have to help him."

The weeks marched slowly on, and as time passed, Chantella felt more like a maid and less and less like her father's daughter.

The twins had started coming home from their shopping trips to the mall or to the city with "gifts" for Chantella.

"I bought you the sweetest outfit today!" Colleen would say, holding up a heavy tan apron to her stepsister's chest.

"I found you a *darling* accessory!" Colin

would say, pulling a feather duster from his shopping bag.

Mara would join in when she was feeling particularly cruel. "This will make your job a lot easier," she would say, laying a toothbrush on Chantella's desk. "Cleaning between the bathroom tiles will be a breeze now."

It was a rainy Saturday in October. The twins and Mara had gone out—to lunch, to a movie, on a shopping spree; it could have been any of those things. Chantella, alone at home, had been assigned to clean the master suite.

Chantella sat on the edge of her father's bed and stared at herself in the mirror on the dresser. Her hair was pulled back, and her eyes were tired and dark. A smudge of dust ran across her cheek. She reached up to wipe the smear away, saw the state of her hands, and thought better of it.

I haven't been in here since before the wedding, she thought. *I haven't seen Dad since that night.*

Chantella sighed, grabbed her bucket that was filled with cans of polish, rags, and dusters, and headed for the suite's double doors, thinking a shower would feel very nice. If she hurried, maybe she'd have time to watch a little television before the stepfamily got home.

But as she reached the doors, they opened. Standing in the doorway was her father.

"Dad!" she said, ready to drop her bucket and throw her arms around him.

Her dad blinked at her and smiled—a smile like he might flash at a familiar face at one of his business gatherings. "Chantella," he said. "I didn't think you'd be in here."

"Oh, I'm just finishing," Chantella said. She sighed loudly and was about to launch into a rant describing all the mistreatment she had suffered at the hands of her stepfamily, but her father rushed past her, loosening his tie.

"What a day," he said. "Nice to come home to a clean bedroom, though." He flashed a

smile at his daughter. "You know," he went on, pulling off his tie and tossing it onto the bed, "I don't think that master bathroom has been cleaned in a while."

"Um . . ." Chantella said. "Dad?"

He must not have heard her, though, or else he chose to ignore her.

"Have Mara and the twins gone out?" he asked.

"Yeah," Chantella said. "They went to a movie or the mall or something."

"Good," he said. "They could use the time to kick back a little. Speaking of kicking back, I'm going to watch some TV and catch up on a few shows. I'll leave you to the bathroom."

With that, he left his daughter standing in his bedroom, bucket of cleaning supplies in hand, and headed downstairs.

"Then it's true," Chantella whispered, shocked. "I'm really the maid."

One fall day, as Thanksgiving approached, and right on its heels, the joyful chaos of Christmas and New Year's Eve, Chantella was enjoying a handful of free minutes in her bedroom. She had a book of music on her lap—a yellowing little paperback her mother had loved to sing songs from—and was settling in to learn a new song before she fell asleep.

As she studied the first song, she heard Mara in the kitchen. "I don't know if Chantella can handle it on her own," her stepmother said.

Chantella closed the book and moved quietly toward the door.

"I have three cousins coming here for Thanksgiving," Mara said, "and then another three for Christmas."

"Where will they all sleep?" Chantella's dad asked. Chantella could tell from his distant voice that he was probably sifting through mail or checking email on his phone while Mara babbled on.

"We'll find a place for everyone in a house this size," Mara said impatiently. "The point is, with Chantella's schoolwork and housework, I fear she won't have time to prepare the kind of meals I feel we ought to serve for the holidays."

"Hmm," her dad said.

"Therefore," Mara went on, "I think the best thing for our family would be to pull Chantella out of school, at least until spring."

"Whatever you think, dear," he said.

She can't be serious! Chantella fumed. *Is he even listening?*

Chantella tore out of her room and into the kitchen. Mara stared her down.

"Anything wrong, girl?" she said.

"Yes!" Chantella snapped. "Dad," she went on, craning her neck to look past Mara where her father was standing with his back to them, "are you really going to let her do this?"

"Hmm?" her father said, not even looking up from his phone. "Whatever you two think is fine with me." Then he left the kitchen.

"There," Mara said, putting her hand on her hip and flashing her pointy teeth at Chantella. "That takes care of that."

"You can't just pull me out of school," Chantella protested. "I'm fifteen. It's illegal."

"Oh, nonsense," Mara said, waving her off. "I'll tell them we're home-schooling. Whatever it takes."

"That is insane!" Chantella said.

"You just worry about that Thanksgiving dinner," Mara said. "I expect a perfect turkey with all the trimmings. You've got a lot of practicing to do, I should think. Have you ever cooked a bird?" Mara didn't wait for a reply. "I'm going upstairs. Mr. Verre doesn't like to be alone for too long. Please turn off the light when you're done straightening up."

Chantella stood in the kitchen, listening to her stepmother's feet on the stairs. Chantella had cried too much. She'd protested too much. She'd cared too much. There was a time—it seemed like forever ago—that her father cared too. That he cried with her. That he screamed at the heavens with her. But he'd changed now, and it seemed he didn't even recognize her.

Chantella couldn't care anymore.

* * *

The holidays were a whirl of hard work and hurt feelings. Chantella collected coats.

She served drinks and passed trays of crackers with cheese, tiny sausages on toothpicks, and asparagus spears wrapped in prosciutto. She ladled out soup, served casseroles, and basted a turkey in November and a goose in December. On New Year's Eve, she filled champagne flutes and swept up broken glass numerous times.

No one was thankful for Chantella. No one hung her stocking over the fireplace. No one wished her a happy holiday.

On December 26th, a red envelope appeared on her bed, though. She tore it open and found a photo of Colleen, Colin, Mara, and her dad standing on the lawn in front of the big snow-covered fir, in their most Christmassy sweaters, each with steaming mugs in their hands and smiles on their faces. Beneath the photo it read: *Happy Holidays from the Verres!*

Chantella tore it up and fell onto her bed in tears.

By the middle of January, Chantella began to realize her stepmother's cruelty was not going to cease with the end of holiday preparations. It seemed Mara would do whatever it took to keep Chantella in her new position as permanent, live-in housekeeper.

She's never going to let me go back to school, Chantella thought as she cleaned the bay windows in the parlor and watched Mara's luxury SUV pull into the circular driveway.

Chantella watched Mara and the twins climb out of the car. It had snowed a little that morning, so a fine dusting still lay on the path from the driveway to the front door.

Mara burst in and snapped, "Chantella!" Then she added more quietly, "Where is that girl?"

Chantella sighed and put down her rags and the bottle of window cleaner. She walked quickly from the parlor to the front door where Mara stood, her arms weighed down by shopping bags. The door was open behind her, and Chantella could see Colleen and Colin on the sloping front yard, quickly gathering snowballs to toss playfully at one another. Their backpacks lay in the driveway, thrown carelessly aside.

"There you are," Mara said, scowling. She didn't even fake a smile. She never did anymore—even when Chantella's dad was around. "What have you been doing, exactly?

I'm sure just sitting around while the house falls apart around you."

Chantella didn't bother to argue. It wouldn't change anything. Besides, Mara barely stopped for a breath. She certainly wasn't expecting an answer to her question.

"You haven't touched the driveway or the paths, and the snow stopped hours ago," Mara said as she kicked off her heels and stalked past Chantella. "Get your shovel and clear the driveway and the paths—and be quick about it. I want supper on the table at six o'clock, sharp!"

Chantella rolled her eyes—she allowed herself that at least—and collected Mara's shoes, scarf, and coat, which Mara had left lying on the floor. She brought them to the closet, put on her heavy coat, grabbed the shovel, and headed outside.

As she walked down the steps to the driveway, an icy snowball struck her in the face.

Colleen and Colin, predictably, cackled like crows.

"Sorry, Chanty," said Colleen, though she wasn't.

The twins grabbed their backpacks and laughed their way past Chantella, into the house, locking the door behind them.

Chantella had a spare key in her coat pocket, but the twins didn't know that.

They're horrible, Chantella thought. *This whole family is horrible.*

She glared toward the door, and in doing so, noticed a fluttering piece of paper on the brick stoop.

"Must have fallen from Colin's backpack," Chantella mumbled as she picked it up.

Next Teen Star is coming to Riverview High School! Are you the next big thing? Come to the auditions this Saturday and show us your stuff!

Chantella held the paper against her chest.

"This could be my chance," she whispered as she shoved the paper into her coat pocket. In a daze of daydreams, she took up the shovel to start the dreary work of clearing the path and driveway.

"I know I'm not as good as Mom was," she muttered, pushing the shovel across the light covering of snow. "But I do have some of her talent, I think."

Chantella passed the time shoveling snow in the dying afternoon light of January, singing to herself.

You are my sunshine, my only sunshine . . .

★ ★ ★

The grandfather clock in the entryway sounded at nine o'clock as Chantella finished cleaning up after dinner. She leaned on the counter and blew her hair out of her eyes.

"The pans have been scrubbed, the dishwasher is running, the table's wiped off and polished, the dining room floor has been swept, and the counters are wiped down and disinfected," she mumbled.

Add that to all the other cleaning and shoveling she'd done, not to mention making and serving the supper, and Chantella was exhausted.

As usual, she thought.

She pulled off her apron and headed for her room to practice a little singing before bed.

On the way, though, she heard the most unusual sound coming down the hallway.

"Is that Colleen?" she wondered aloud.

There was no one else it could be, but while Colleen often talked quite loudly—and laughed and cackled and shrieked and demanded and snarled and snapped and belittled and swore— she certainly never sang.

Chantella quietly moved down the hallway toward the living room.

She stopped, just out of sight, and held her

breath. It was definitely Colleen singing, and a moment later Colin joined her.

They're singing a duet! Or trying to, at least. Chantella thought, amused and very confused.

They kept cutting off each other's parts and messing up the words. Their voices weren't terrible, though. Better than Chantella would have guessed from listening to their unbearable speaking voices.

When they finished the song, the twins immediately began snapping at one another.

"You stepped on my cue!"

"You missed the harmony in the first reprise!"

"You blew the key change in the middle eight!"

"You sing like a dying cat!"

At that point, it must have turned into a physical fight, because Mara—who had apparently been observing—finally spoke up.

"Enough, enough!" she shouted. "You were both atrocious. If you're to have any chance of passing the audition on Saturday and getting on that show—and winning the grand prize money and recording contract and tour—you'd better worry more about how to get better instead of which of you is worse."

They began shrieking at each other again, and Chantella took advantage of the loud distraction to hurry to her room so she could practice as well.

On Saturday morning, Chantella searched the house for her father, practicing her audition song as she looked for him and straightened up. Perhaps he wasn't the father he should have been, or the father he once was, but he was more her parent than Mara was.

"If I could just find him," she told herself, "he'd let me go to the audition."

It may have been true—it may not have been true. It didn't matter. Chantella searched high and low all over the Verre mansion and never found him.

"Please," Chantella finally said when she came across Mara sitting in the parlor. "Let me come to the audition today."

"You?" Mara said, a look of disgust and disbelief on her face.

Chantella nodded firmly.

Mara sighed. "Very well," she said. "If you've finished your chores for the morning, you may come to support your brother and sister. It might do them good to have someone rooting for them."

Chantella felt her face redden. "No, Mara," she said. "That's not what I mean. I want to sing. I want to audition."

Mara shot to her feet as if a pin had just burst up from the cushion of her seat and poked her in the butt. "Audition?!" she snapped. "I have never heard such arrogance in my life!"

The twins, alerted by their mother's shouting, ran into the parlor.

"This uppity child," Mara told them, "seems to think *she* carries some kind of vocal talent within that plain face of hers."

The twins laughed cruelly.

"Do you think, girl," Mara went on, glaring at Chantella, "that because *some* people thought your mother had a smidgen of musical skill, that they'll think *you* contain something special?"

Chantella didn't respond. She didn't shake her head, and she didn't scream in Mara's face, though she wanted to. Instead, she just stared at her feet.

"Mom," Colleen said, running to Mara's side and grabbing her arm pleadingly. "Let her come. Let her sing. She'll embarrass herself!"

Colin cheered for the idea, but Mara didn't even smile. Chantella could read her face: Mara knew very well that Chantella's mother could sing beautifully, and she worried that Chantella could sing, too.

She's worried I'll be competition for her horrible twins, Chantella thought. She wanted to grin, but held back.

"Very well," Mara said, her voice now calm, but cold. "You may come to the audition . . . if you finish all your chores."

"I have, Mara," Chantella said. "I finished all my Saturday chores this morning."

"Today," Mara said, pacing in front of Chantella, "is a *special* Saturday. Since both of the twins will be busy today, they won't have time to focus on their homework."

Chantella held her breath. Was Mara about to say what she thought she might say? "Finish their homework," her stepmother said. "If you're done by noon—when we're leaving— you may join us."

Chantella could hardly breathe, but she didn't protest. She didn't shriek at them. She just stomped one foot and huffed out of the room.

"I'll bring you my math and history handouts!" Colleen called after her.

Chantella ran to her room and slammed the door behind her. She fell face-first onto her bed and wailed.

"I can't take it anymore!" Chantella cried into her pillow to muffle the sound. "It's too unfair. Too impossible. How can I possibly go on like this any longer?"

"Perhaps you can go a teensy bit longer," said a familiar voice from behind her.

Chantella turned around. There, seated and smiling, with her legs crossed at the ankles and her hands folded in her lap, was Chantella's former nanny—and the former resident of this very room.

"Verna!" Chantella shouted. "What are you doing here?" She leaped from the bed and hugged her tightly.

"Shh!" Verna said with a little laugh. "I don't want your mother and siblings to know I'm here."

"They aren't my mother and my siblings," Chantella said, releasing her former nanny. "How did you get in here?"

Verna opened her hands to reveal a set of keys. "I've held on to these," she admitted. "I suppose I shouldn't have. But when I saw you at the wedding, I was glad I did."

Chantella nodded. "And *I'm* glad you did," she said. "I'm having the worst time, and I've had no one to talk to."

But now she did. Chantella let it all out—everything that had happened since she last saw Verna at the wedding. When she finished the whole horrible story, Verna's jaw hung open in shock.

"We must do something to fix this," Verna said. "But for the moment, let's just get you to that audition."

"How?" Chantella said. "Mara won't let me go unless I do her bratty kids' homework."

"Then we will do their homework," Verna said matter-of-factly.

Suddenly, they heard a knock. "Our homework for you!" Colin called through the closed door. "And you better hurry! We're dying to see you screw up that audition!"

He and Colleen laughed as they retreated down the stairs. Verna stood up, opened the door, collected the books and notebooks, and brought them inside. She flipped through the assignments, nodding and clucking her teeth.

"I think," she said, "if we split this work, we'll finish in no time."

* * *

"Hurry, now!" Verna said. It was 11:55, and the twins' homework was done. While Verna touched up the last few math problems, Chantella had practically thrown herself into her blue dress and white flats—the only outfit she owned that seemed nice enough for an audition for *Next Teen Star.*

Verna pressed the twins' books into Chantella's arms and practically shoved her out of the room. "She'll leave without you if you don't hurry!" Verna said.

"I'm going, I'm going!" Chantella said, smiling as she hurried down the hall. "Mara! Mara! I've finished the work!"

She ran to the front door, where Mara and the twins, with their coats and scarves on and looks of anxious excitement on their faces, were about to leave for the audition.

Mara glanced over Chantella's shoulder at the grandfather clock. "You almost didn't make it in time," she said, faking a smile—as if she'd wanted Chantella to join them.

Chantella passed the stack of textbooks and notebooks to the twins. Colin flipped through some pages, examining the work. He shrugged and said, "Looks like she actually did it all."

Colleen perused her stack as well. But then she said, "Wait a second. Where's the paper on fairy tales?"

Chantella's heart pounded hard against her ribs and then seemed to stop. "Paper?" she said. "You didn't say anything about a paper on fairy tales."

"Oh, didn't I?" Colleen said, dropping the stack of homework onto a table in the entryway. "Must have slipped my mind."

Mara looked delighted. She laughed and patted her daughter on the head as the three left the front door standing open, letting a cold breeze waft into the house as they went outside and climbed into the SUV.

Chantella barely dragged herself back to her room. She should have been furious. She should have been stomping through the house like a goddess of rage and destruction, tearing Mara's art from the walls, smashing mirrors, and gashing cushions and upholstery.

But she was too exhausted. Instead of rage, she felt sorrow and exhaustion. Chantella collapsed on her bed. She might have fallen asleep if Verna hadn't come into the room a moment later.

"What are you doing here?" Verna asked, sitting beside Chantella on the bed. She felt her nanny's comforting hand on her back. "Shouldn't you be halfway there by now?"

Chantella rolled onto her back and held up the crumpled paper. "We didn't do it all," she said. "There was one more assignment: an essay on fairy tales. Colleen tricked us."

"Well, fairy tales will be easy," she said. "I happen to know quite a bit about them. I can write this."

Chantella shrugged. "What's the point?" she said. "I'd have to leave right now to make it to the auditions on time."

"And leave right now you shall," Verna said. "I'll drive you."

Chantella sat up. "They'll want to know if I've finished the paper," she said.

"Then you'll tell them you have," Verna said. "You'll tell them it's typed up neatly and that you've put it on Colleen's desk. They'll find it there when you get back."

Chantella had her doubts about this plan, but it was worth a try. She got up from the bed and checked herself in the mirror.

"Oh, I've ruined my makeup," she said. "And my dress is a wrinkled mess!"

Verna shook her head. "You can't go like that," she said. She thought for a moment, humming, and then snapped her fingers. "You fix your makeup—I have the perfect idea for a dress. I'll be right back."

Chantella went to her bathroom to freshen up. She heard Verna's fast footsteps on the stairs. When she'd finished, she heard Verna's footsteps rushing back downstairs.

"I found it!" she called. "I found it!"

Her nanny hurried into Chantella's room, holding a tall, black garment bag.

"What is that?" Chantella said as Verna laid it on the bed.

"I wasn't sure it would still be here," Verna said, smiling. "I thought for sure Mara would have found it and destroyed it. But it was just where she'd left it."

"She?" Chantella said. She had an idea she knew who Verna meant, but it was too good to believe.

Verna unzipped the bag and pulled out a dress. It was shimmering white silk, long and strapless, with a black ribbon around the waist. Chantella recognized it at once.

"Mom," she said in a hushed whisper.

She hurried to pull her secret stash of photos from under her bed and found it right away: her mom, only a few years older than Chantella, wearing the same dress onstage.

"It's the first night Dad met Mom," Chantella said, staring at the photo. "He took this photo that night, and he introduced himself after the concert. He says he couldn't help himself."

Verna nodded and smiled. "I've heard that story," she said. "Your mom told it to me a hundred times."

Chantella wiped a tear from her cheek.

"Put it on," Verna said. "Quickly."

* * *

"It's perfect," Chantella said, standing in front of the mirror and smiling at her reflection.

"Good," Verna said. "But we don't have time to gape at you, even if you do look as beautiful as your mother. We have to get going."

Chantella stepped into her shoes and hurried with Verna to the front door.

As they were gathering their coats, just about to leave the house, the door flew open, letting in an icy January wind and blowing snow. And suddenly, there was Chantella's red-faced father, bundled up in layers.

He stopped inside the doorway, standing there on the doormat, staring at Chantella. It seemed like he barely noticed their former nanny.

"Dad," Chantella said.

"What is this?" he said after a moment. "Where are you going? Why are you wearing that dress?"

"Don't be angry," Chantella said. She stepped toward him and held one of his frigid hands. "Verna knew where to find it, and it's absolutely perfect."

Her father could only nod.

"I feel as if I haven't seen you in a very long time," he said.

"You haven't," Chantella said.

He shook his head. "That's not what I mean," he said. "I mean . . ." It seemed like he couldn't find the words he wanted.

Chantella didn't let him finish. She didn't need to. She wrapped her arms around his waist, and he held her against him. "I've been a horrible father," he finally said, with his face pressed to the top of her head.

"Yes, you have," said Verna as she put a coat over Chantella's shoulders. "But now we really must go if your daughter is to make it to the audition on time."

"The audition," her dad said, lifting his head. "Yes, the twins mentioned something about that." He looked at Chantella again. "That's why you're wearing your mom's dress. It's perfect on you."

"Then you don't mind if I go?" she asked.

"Don't mind?" her dad said. "Honey, of course! You *must* audition. In fact, for the last few days, as I've listened to the twins talk about it constantly—I don't think I like them at all, by the way. They're always talking, aren't they?—I had the most frustrating feeling of trying to figure something out, but I couldn't figure out what."

"Like you'd been under a spell?" Verna said mysteriously.

Chantella's father's face lit up, as if he was seeing her for the first time. "Verna!" he said. "That's it exactly! And now I see what it was that troubled me—the wrong children were auditioning."

"In fact, Chantella was doing their homework for them," Verna added with a little venom in her voice. "Not to mention acting as their maid."

Her dad gave Chantella a sharp look. "Is this true?" he said.

Chantella nodded. She told him about Mara's cruelty and described what she and Verna had been up to that morning, completing the twins' homework assignments so she could get to the audition.

"Enough, enough!" Verna pleaded. "You'll start crying again and ruin your makeup—again! We really must go." She nudged Chantella out the door.

"Just a minute," her dad said. "We'll take my car. If you're driving that little hatchback I saw in the driveway, I'd say we'll fare better in the snow in my SUV."

The three hurried out to Mr. Verre's car.

"And believe me," he said as they hopped in the car, "Mara has a lot to answer for."

~10~

Chantella's dad's SUV screeched up to the curb in front of Riverview High School.

"You'd better hurry," he said to his daughter. "If that flyer is right, they're closing the sign-up sheet in just a few minutes."

"Thanks, Dad," Chantella said. She leaned over and kissed his cheek as Verna jumped from the backseat, threw open Chantella's door, and grabbed her hand.

"Good luck!" her dad called. "I'll find a place to park!"

Chantella let Verna lead her, running through the empty halls of the school. She could hear music coming down the hall from the auditorium.

"The auditions are starting!" Verna said, tugging at Chantella's wrist. "Come on!"

They reached the auditorium. In front of the closed double doors was a long table strewn with clipboards and pens. There, organizing the papers and clipboards into piles, stood a young man in a bright blue suit.

"Are we too late?" Verna said, but the man wasn't looking at her. He was looking at Chantella.

"My goodness," he said, awestruck. "You're the spitting image of the great singer, Cordelia Verre. Her voice was as pure and clear as glass."

Chantella felt herself blushing. "I'm her—" she began, but Verna cut her off.

"Can she still sign up?" Verna said.

"Oh," the young man replied. "To audition? Of course. Do you have background music?"

Chantella pushed her CD across the table, and the man handed her a clipboard.

"Thanks," Chantella said as she filled in the sign-up sheet.

When Chantella finished filling it out, she and Verna hurried to the "green room," which was really just a pair of science classrooms adjacent to the auditorium.

Inside, they found chaos. Dozens of teens sat and stood and leaped and danced and sang all over the room.

Standing face-to-face by the windows, with Mara behind them, were the twins. They spotted Chantella right away. Colleen tapped her mother's elbow and nodded at Chantella. Mara curled her lip and stalked through the crowd toward Chantella.

"Uh-oh," Chantella said. "Here she comes. And if you're here with me, you're obviously not working on that paper for Colleen. Mara is going to kill me."

"Working on it?" Verna said. She opened her bag and pulled out a thick, stapled booklet labeled *On Fairy Tales, by Colleen Verre.*

"I did it in the car on the way here," Verna said. She handed Chantella the paper.

Chantella faced Verna in surprise. "In the car?" she said. "But it's typed. How did you—?"

"What are you doing here?" Mara snapped at Chantella. "I made it very clear that you were not to come down here unless you'd finished your work."

Chantella held up the paper. "Done," she said, pressing it into Mara's hands. "Excuse me," she said as she stepped around Mara and walked away. Verna hurried to keep up.

"That was awesome," Verna said.

"I'm shaking like a leaf," Chantella said.

"You did great," Verna said.

At that moment, the door at the back of the room opened, and the young man in blue stuck his head inside. "Colleen and Colin, twins duet!" he shouted. "You're up!"

★ ★ ★

Chantella and Verna stood near the doors to listen to the twins' performance.

"They're not that bad, actually," Chantella said.

"They *do* have nice voices," Verna admitted. "Especially Colleen."

"Still," Chantella said, "they don't exactly work well together."

They couldn't see the stage. They could only hear the vocals. But the way the twins kept singing over each other, and with the commotion from the audience, it sure seemed like—

"I think she pushed him!" Verna whispered excitedly. "Is that possible?"

Chantella covered her mouth to stifle a laugh as the song finished.

A moment later, Mara stormed into the green room, the look on her face revealing everything. The twins hadn't done well.

* * *

They were well into the fourth hour of auditions when Chantella's name was finally called.

"You're up," the man in the blue suit said as he walked toward her. He smiled.

Chantella squeezed Verna's hand and followed the young man out to the stage.

"What's your name?" called a voice from the front of the dark auditorium—it must have been one of the judges.

Chantella shielded her eyes and squinted against the spotlight, trying to see them.

"Chantella Verre." The microphone squealed, and she stepped back a little. "Sorry."

"Whenever you're ready," one of the judges said, and Chantella's background track began.

She listened to the familiar strains of piano, the whispering of snare drums, and a double bass that sounded like gentle ocean waves. And she began to sing.

∿11∿

The crowd—small though it was—went
wild. Chantella beamed and bowed.
The house lights came up, and she spotted
her father, near the front and on his feet. He
whistled and clapped and hollered.

"Thank you," said a judge, and Chantella
hurried off the stage.

The young man in the blue suit took her
hand. "You were amazing," he said to her. "It
was like watching Cordelia." He sniffed and

wiped a tear from his eye. "Your last name is Verre? You must be her daughter."

Chantella nodded. "I am," she said, and she found she was crying, too.

"You'll win for sure," he whispered.

Her father waited for her in the green room—along with Verna, Mara, and the twins.

"My little girl!" her dad exclaimed, throwing his arms around her. "You were amazing."

Chantella could have stayed in that hug forever. But they weren't alone. They were surrounded by a pair of horrid twins and their wicked mother.

"Stop this ridiculousness at once!" Mara snapped, trying to pull her husband away from Chantella. "This girl *deliberately* disobeyed me by coming here."

Chantella's dad turned and faced Mara. "You," he said. "You've been a beast. So have your disgusting, bratty children."

Mara gasped. "How dare you!" she said. "You are my husband, and I will *not* have my husband speak to me like this."

"You certainly won't," her dad went on, matching her rage, and shouting just as loud. "The way you've treated my daughter over the past few months has been too awful."

Several performers, two of the judges, and the young man in the blue suit turned to watch the spectacle.

"Ha!" Mara said, stomping her foot. "As if you cared. You treated her as bad as any of us."

"Dad," Chantella said. She tugged at her father's sleeve. "Please stop shouting. Everyone's watching."

He ignored her. It reminded her of the recent months since the wedding, when he ignored her all the time, and it stung. Her eyes filled with tears.

"That's over as of today," her dad said to Mara. "And so is this marriage. I want you out."

Mara gasped. "I'll sue!" she shouted. "I'll take you for everything you're worth!"

Chantella was thrilled to witness the marriage crumbling right before her eyes. But she couldn't take the shouting anymore. Especially with all these people watching. With tears streaming down her face, she ran from the green room.

"Chantella!" Verna called after her. "Wait!"

"Sweetheart!" her dad called.

"Please!" shouted a third voice. "Don't leave!"

But Chantella didn't care. The day had been too much: too much emotion, too much work, too much remembering her mom and dad and how their family had once been. She burst through the doors of Riverview High School and hugged herself tight. The snow blew through the parking lot, blinding her, so she huddled against the side of the building and sobbed.

~ 12 ~

"I'm sorry about that scene," Chantella's dad said after driving in silence for several minutes.

Chantella sat in the back of the SUV with Verna, who had showed up outside just a moment after Chantella realized how stupid she'd been to run out into the cold January afternoon in a strapless dress without a coat.

"You didn't need to run off like that, though," her dad went on.

The SUV rushed along the winding streets up the hillside toward the Verre mansion. As they pulled into the driveway, Chantella saw Mara's SUV already parked there, and she groaned.

Verna patted her arm. "It's almost over," she said. "The story has just one more chapter."

The car stopped, and Chantella's father hurried to open the door for her. She took his hand and held it as they walked inside and settled into the kitchen, trying to avoid Mara.

"I'm going to change into something more comfortable," Chantella said, feeling exhausted.

Chantella hoped Verna was right. She hoped the story was almost over. It hadn't been a very good story, but an end would at least be an end.

* * *

Chantella showered and pulled on the jeans and T-shirt she always wore to do housework. They weren't glamorous, like her mother's dress. They weren't impressive, like the satin shoes she should never have worn in the snow. But they *were* very comfortable.

Chantella sat down with a sigh. She might have laid on the bed . . . slept until the divorce was final and the horrible stepfamily had moved out. But then she heard the deep tones of the doorbell.

"Someone else will get it," she muttered. After all, with her dad back in his right mind and Mara and the twins on their way out, Chantella wasn't the maid anymore.

But the excited shouts and hurrying feet made her curious. With a groan, Chantella got up from the bed and dragged herself out of the maid's quarters and into the living area.

"Please, sit here," Colleen shouted to the guest, excited and overly courteous.

Chantella couldn't see who it was, though, with the soon-to-divorce Verres hovering around him.

"Can I get you something hot to drink?" Colin said. "You must be freezing after your journey."

"Yes!" Mara said. "Get him some tea."

"Enough!" the man said, leaping from the chair. "I don't want to sit. I don't want any tea. I'm just looking for a singer at this address!"

Chantella gasped. It was the man who was working at the *Next Teen Star* audition! His suit was as blue and startling as she remembered.

"It seems someone found my clipboard and tore the papers to pieces," the man began. "And we're having a heck of a time figuring out which singer goes with which number and which address. All we know is that she was the daughter of the great singer Cordelia Verre, and her voice was as pure and clear as glass— like her mother's."

"We auditioned!" Colleen said, stepping up to the man, flashing a smile and batting her eyelashes.

The young man peered at her. He pulled a pair of glasses from his jacket pocket, put them on, and peered at her again.

"Hmm," he said. "You look familiar. But . . . I don't know."

"*She's* the girl you're looking for," Mara said, hurrying forward and squeezing Colleen's shoulder. "Voice like an angel!"

She smiled and whispered in Colleen's ear, "Sing for him, my darling."

Colleen's eyes went wide with fear, but she recovered quickly, cleared her throat, and began to sing. She only sang her parts, though. Duets sound awfully funny with just one person.

"Wait a minute," the man said. Colleen stopped. "Do you have a partner for this song?" He scanned the room.

For the briefest moment, the man's eyes fell upon Chantella. He paused. Chantella lifted her chin and smiled, but in her housework clothes, she was unrecognizable to him.

"My brother!" Colleen said, grabbing her twin by the wrist. "He's my partner."

The twins nodded at each other, counted to four, and began to sing together.

"Stop, stop!" the man in blue shouted. "I recognize you both! I recognize your song!"

Colleen and Colin stopped, somehow still grinning and hopeful.

"He recognizes us," Colin said, stars in his eyes.

"We'll be famous!" Colleen swooned, her hands clasped to her heart.

"I recognize you because your act was so remarkably painful to watch," the man said. "You step on each other's cues. You constantly try to outdo each other. You sound more like a *duel* than a duet!"

Exasperated, he reached into his pocket and pulled out a torn and crumpled sheet of paper. He squinted at the ink on it and said, "Does anyone else live here? Another teen singer who auditioned today?"

"No one!" Mara shouted, stepping in front of Chantella. "My twins, whom you've so rudely insulted this afternoon, are the only ones!"

Just then, Verna and Chantella's father, who had heard the commotion from the kitchen, hurried into the living room.

"Hmm," the man said again, trying to peek past Mara, "who is that, then?" He peered toward Chantella.

"That's my daughter," Chantella's dad said. "She aud—"

"The maid!" Mara said, cutting him off. "She's just the maid."

"Nonsense!" Verna said, nudging Mara aside. "She's not the maid. This is more her house than it is theirs." She waved dismissively toward the twins.

"Maid or not," the man in blue said, "makes no difference to me. If she can sing, I want to hear it."

"Waste of time!" Mara shouted as Chantella stepped forward. "And who are *you* anyway?" she growled to Verna.

"A family friend," Verna said simply.

"What should we do?" Colleen whispered to Colin, but he just shrugged.

Then Chantella took a deep breath and stepped forward. Her heart pounded. Her skin tingled. Then she clasped her fingers together and began to sing.

The man's stern mouth turned into a gentle smile. His eyes, which before were almost disdainful, softened.

Chantella sang an entire song for him, feeling less nervous and more confident as she went. When she finished the refrain, the man clapped his hands.

"Beautiful," he said. "Your voice is every bit the voice of your mother's. I'd know it anywhere—even if I didn't recognize you when you weren't wearing that beautiful dress."

"Thank you," Chantella said.

The man picked up his coat and got ready to leave. "I suppose it goes without saying," he said. "You've won this audition. You're off to Hollywood, then!" Chantella couldn't speak. She smiled and hugged him.

"We'll be in touch soon," he said. "My name is Brendan Charmant, and I'm the producer of *Next Teen Star*. Contact me if you need anything at all," he said as he left. Chantella waved from the doorway as his sleek black car pulled out of the driveway.

Mara faced Chantella, her father, and Verna with an evil look on her face. "This changes nothing," she said. "I'll take you for everything you're worth. The house. The cars. I'll get you for alimony till the day you die!"

"Alimony?" Verna said. "You've been married less than six months!"

Chantella's dad stood up straight, a peaceful and triumphant look on his face. "You know what, Mara?" he said. "You want the house? The cars? Take 'em."

"Dad!" Chantella said, horrified.

"My girl and I," her dad said, taking Chantella's hands in his, "are going to Hollywood, and we're not looking back."

"You mean it?" Chantella said. She could hardly believe it.

Her dad nodded. "It's what I should have done for your mother years ago, but I was obsessed with my business and money instead."

Chantella hugged him. "Can we bring Verna with us?" she asked.

Her dad shrugged. "I suppose," he said.

They both looked around the living room, but the nanny was gone.

~13~

Chantella and her father rented a small house in the Hollywood Hills. Since her father didn't put up any fight about money or property, the divorce was final quickly.

Chantella came in second in the national *Next Teen Star* competition. She lost in the very final round to an opera singer from Alaska. He was an impressive musician, Chantella had to admit.

And the "Girl with the Glass Voice," as

Chantella came to be known on the show, was a huge hit with the audience. Her performance in the *Next Teen Star* finale, though it didn't win, got over a million views online in just two weeks.

The producer of the show, Brendan Charmant, had so much faith in her talent that he quit his job at *Next Teen Star* to become her manager, booking performances and meet-and-greets for her all around the country and preparing to sign a contract with a top record company for her first album.

If you watched the video of Chantella's final performance very carefully—which Chantella often did—you could see a young woman in the front row of the audience. She was wearing a bright-green dress and a matching hat with a green feather in it, and she was the first person on her feet when Chantella finished her performance.

Chantella watched the video over and over

just to see that woman: Verna, her former nanny, whom Chantella hadn't been able to track down since moving to Hollywood.

Maybe one day—someday when Chantella needed her more than anything—Verna would pop in again like a fairy godmother and grant her all her wishes.

But for now, living happily in California with her dad, Chantella felt like all her wishes had come true.

With Brendan teaching her the ropes of the singing business, Chantella quickly became popular throughout the country. Brendan booked her on a national tour that began immediately after her work for *Next Teen Star* wrapped up. Chantella's show in her hometown is already sold out.

Cinderella

• ★ • ★ •

Cinderella, or *The Little Glass Slipper* as it is also known, is a popular tale throughout the world, the foundation of which has given life to thousands of different versions. All of the tales feature a young woman living in the midst of cruelty and poverty, whose luck, by the end of the story, suddenly changes for the better.

The earliest version of the story with which we are probably most familiar was *Cenerentola*, written by Giambattista Basile and published in 1634. This story featured a young woman, Zezolla, whose father was a widowed prince. He marries the governess of the palace, but after they marry, the governess becomes evil. She and her six daughters abuse Zezolla and treat her as their servant.

The prince meets a fairy who gives him gifts for his daughter: a golden bucket and spade, a silk napkin, and a date seed. Zezolla plants the seed. When it eventually grows into a tree, Zezolla finds a fairy living in it.

When the king throws a ball, the fairy helps Zezolla dress in beautiful clothes. The king falls in love with Zezolla at the ball, but she flees him and his guards on three separate occassions. The third time she runs away, she loses one of her slippers. The king finds it and invites all the women in the kingdom to a feast so he can see whose foot best fits the shoe. When Zezolla arrives, however, the shoe magically jumps from the king's hand to her foot. They marry and live happily ever after.

A later version of the story, written by Charles Perrault in 1697, is even more familiar to readers in the United States as it includes the fairy-godmother figure, the glass slipper, and the pumpkin.

Tell your own Twicetold Tale!

• ★ • ★ •

Choose one from each group, and write a story that combines all of the elements you've chosen.

A warrior who travels the world

A prince who refuses to wear fancy clothes

A queen who loves to eat chocolate

A goblin who is teased

A safe

A fancy hat

An orange tree

A silver plate

A gazebo in a park

A toolshed

An old house

A castle by the sea

A brilliant boy

A sleepy elf

A kindly king

A grumpy giant

A deer

A shark

A unicorn

A seagull

Texas

The North Pole

Ireland

Chicago

about the author

Olivia Snowe lives between the falls, the forest, and the creek in Minneapolis, Minnesota.

about the illustrator

Michelle Lamoreaux is an illustrator from southern Utah. She works with many publishers, agencies, and magazines throughout the US. She currently works out of Salt Lake City, Utah.